BEYOND TOMORROW

TOKI MATSUDAIRA

Copyright @2023 by Toki Matsudaira

All rights reserved. No part of this book may be reproduced in any form or by any electronic or mechanical means, including information storage and retrieval systems, without permission in writing from the publisher, except by reviewers, who may quote brief passages in a review.

This publication contains the opinions and ideas of its author. It is intended to provide helpful and informative material on the subjects addressed in the publication. The author and publisher specifically disclaim all responsibility for any liability, loss or risk, personal or otherwise, which is incurred as a consequence, directly or indirectly, of the use and application of any of the contents of this book.

WORKBOOK PRESS LLC
187 E Warm Springs Rd,
Suite B285, Las Vegas, NV 89119, USA

Website:	https://workbookpress.com/
Hotline:	1-888-818-4856
Email:	admin@workbookpress.com

Ordering Information:
Quantity sales. Special discounts are available on quantity purchases by corporations, associations, and others. For details, contact the publisher at the address above.

Library of Congress Control Number:

ISBN-13: 978-1-960752-65-9 (Paperback Version)
          978-1-960752-66-6 (Digital Version)

REV. DATE: 02/16/2023

BEYOND TOMORROW

It was within the confines of these garden walls when I saw Georgia. She was standing by a bed of white flowers and stooping down to pick some roses, she noticed me.

"Oh, you gave me a fright!" she exclaimed. "I didn't know you were there". I offered her a helping hand as she rose to get up. She walked across the garden to a bench where she sat down.

I followed her and she sat down next to me.

It was a cloudy day, but the sun did come out intermittently which improved our mood. Georgia loved her garden and in the spring she planted many flowers.

I am Kevin, Kevin Wilson. I live and work as a travel agent in an office in Victoria, in London. I had come down to the Manor House just outside Tunbridge Wells, for the weekend and Georgia Gibson was my hostess. We sat quietly on the bench, neither of us saying much to each other. Finally, Georgia asked me "And how are you?"

"O.K. I guess" I replied.

She looked tired that afternoon and the dark circles under her eyes proved that she was very busy and worked hard in the house. I said nothing except "you're looking well. And how is Alan?

"Oh, he's good" she said. "Not getting any younger but getting by nicely." She explained." Have the servants shown you your room" she asked. I told her my suitcase was there but that I had not yet started unpacking.

"I wanted to find you before I settled in." "I had a hunch you might be in the garden" I explained.

"Did you drive or come by train?" she asked. "I drove" I said.

"How long was the journey?" she asked.

"About two hours from London" I said. "You must be thirsty" she said. "Come let us go in and we'll find some tea for you. She got up slowly and we both walked to the gate of the garden. We walked onto a gravel path to the main house and entered by the front door. She quickly changed shoes by the front door and walked across to the study before ordering tea. She left briefly for the kitchen to put the roses into water. She must not have been gone for more than four minutes. When she returned she had the roses in a vase filled with water. She placed it on a side table next to the sofa. They smelled fresh from the garden and gave over a lovely scent. Soon tea was brought in with a cake their cook had made. She poured the tea into cups and added milk in each cup. She cut a piece of cake and placed it on a plate with a fork and gave it to me. She then cut a piece of it for herself. In the course of consuming our tea and cake, Georgia referred to Alan's new car, a Mercedes coupe. She told me how he loved driving it. He had to go to the Post Office which explained why he wasn't there to greet him.

"This evening, we have invited Theresa who is the daughter of our neighbour the

Cunninghams. You'll meet Alan over cocktails this evening at about 6. "Oh, by the way, how old are you?"

"I'm forty" I said. "That's perfect, because Theresa is in her late twenties. We will only be four tonight. Sunday, we will give a lunch party. We will probably have it on the terrace, weather permitting. Georgia then looked at her watch and said she would be late unless they went now to their rooms to change for dinner. As she got up from the sofa I rose and thanked her for the wonderful tea. It was now 5pm. "We'll meet in the study at 6.30 for cocktails. Alan will be there at 6. You can join him then. She walked out of the study and went up the stairs. I followed her and went to my room where I would unpack and change for dinner with a shower in mind.

CHAPTER 2

I went down to the sitting room just after 6. Nothing had changed. Alan was preparing himself a gin martini cocktail and when he saw me he put down the cocktail shaker to come up to me to shake my hand saying "Good to see you again, Kevin old boy." After asking me how the journey went and did I remember from the last time, how to find the house, he went back to the bar and poured the martini cocktail into a cocktail glass. "Do you want the same thing?" he asked me "Yes, that would be nice" I replied. We both stood by the bar while he prepared another martini. When finished, he offered me a glass. "Come let us sit down" he said. He chose to sit on an armchair and waved a seat on the sofa near his chair. He raised his glass saying "Welcome back to the Manor House. We then sipped the drink. There were almonds on a small silver dish on the side table. Alan picked it up and offered them to me. I took some.

He wanted to take a trip to the Far East to visit Japan. he said "We wanted to ask you if you could do an itinerary of a tour there and advise us on hotels. We heard that in Kyoto there is an excellent Japanese inn which is meant to be the best hotel in Kyoto.

Naturally we would have to sleep on the floor on a futon and eat only Japanese food in the room. Could you check this out? We want a guided tour of Kyoto and see all the sights. We want to see Nara as well. That is quite close to Kyoto.

We wanted to go to Japan when the cherry blossoms are out." That would be in March, Sir I explained. There is also the Isu Peninsular in the southern part of the mainland we'd love to see and also the famous Modern Museum on

Naoshima Island. We would have to spend a few nights there in their hotel. We want to be in Japan for three weeks. Can you arrange all this for us?

"Anything is possible" I said. Just then Georgia walked in and greeted the two men." I'll get you a drink" said Alan. "One gin and tonic coming up" he said. Georgia joined her husband at the bar and waited for her drink. It was now 7 and just then walked in who I presumed to be Theresa. After the introduction, she sat down on the sofa next to me. She was a slim girl with blond hair and blue eyes.

After being given a drink of martini cocktail, Georgia and Alan asked her how her parents were and what they were up to these days. Replying to their questions, she momentarily forgot her drink. After the interrogation she remembered her cocktail and sipped it enjoying it. At 7.30 the butler came into the Drawing Room and addressed us saying "Dinner is served." We all got up and followed our host and hostess into the Dining Room. Out host took the seat next to Theresa, while I was seated next to Georgia. The butler came in and proceeded to pour white wine into our wine glasses. Alan lifted his glass of wine and said "To your health and let us hope you will return to us more frequently when you are able to get out of London." We took our glasses and drank some of the wine. "It is a very good bottle" said Alan. It is a Chablis.

Over dinner I talked to Georgia about their future trip to Japan. I asked her if they had any date in mind next March when the cherry blossoms would start to bloom. "When do they come out? Is it the first week or the second week of March?" she asked. I replied that the second week of March should be a good time to be in Tokyo for the cherry blossoms. "I haven't much experience about travelling in Japan and will book it all with a tour operator" I said.

I then turned to Theresa who was sitting silently eating her dinner of fish. "Do you live in the country all the time or do you live in London,?" I asked her. I'm only down here for the week-end to help out in the garden" she explained. I normally live in London. " I have a job as a shop assistant at Prada, in Bond Street." "So you're in the fashion trade" I exclaimed. "Yes" she said. "Do they do men's fashion as well?" I asked. "It's exclusively ladies wear". she explained.

Alan cut in just then saying "My daughter Jane shops there and recently bought a yellow silk printed dress which Theresa helped her chose. I can't say I like all the new fashion but I thought her Prada dress was beautiful. Her husband Gary was pleased with the purchase which he paid for. They are not necessarily among the very wealthy but it was a special present for her from Gary. He took her out to dinner that evening. Very decent of him. After dessert we got up from the table and walked back into the Drawing Room for coffee.

Neither Alan or Georgia smoked. We were in the middle of drinking coffee when the butler came in offering us liqueurs." I suggest you have a brandy" Alan said to me.

And turning to Theresa, asked her what she'd like. "An Amaretto with ice, if you have it." she said. John the butler said there was a full bottle. He turned to Georgia who said she would have the same thing for a change away from the cherry herring she usually drank after dinner. In a few minutes, John carried a tray of the drinks offering them to us.

After we had finished our liqueurs Theresa got up" and said "What a lovely evening it's been. So good to see you both. I hope your plans for Japan will be marvellous. Anyway, I'll see you both on Sunday. Turning to me, she said "nice meeting you." "Perhaps we can meet up in London sometime "I said. "I'll get your details from Georgia". "That sounds great" she said. "I'll look forward to that."

It was still cold outside that April evening, and she hastily put on her black coat John helped her into. She waved goodbye as she stepped out the front door. It had gone 10.30. The grand-father clock in the hall chimed the half hour while the door closed and we went back to the Drawing Room. I felt very sleepy all of a sudden and made my exit from Georgia and Alan bidding them a good-night and telling them what a wonderful evening it had been. Georgia came up to me and kissed me on the cheek and Alan stood by and wished me a good night. I left the room and made my way upstairs to my bedroom.

I was soundly asleep when I heard a noise in my room. I turned on the bed side light but didn't see anything. I looked at my watch and saw that it was two in the morning. I kept the light on for a few minutes longer but as nothing seemed disturbed, I turned them off and went back to sleep.

In the morning I looked around the room and noticed that my briefcase was open. I checked it and found some papers missing mainly the itineraries of several clients who had made bookings to go abroad. I looked for them everywhere in the room and inspected my suitcase but they were nowhere to be found. Little did I suspect that the flight details and hotel information were of interest to somebody. I looked at my watch and saw that it had gone a few minutes past 8.

I changed and went down for breakfast. I was the first to come in. John the butler came in and seated me by the window and asked me if I wanted coffee or tea. I asked for coffee. He explained that there was a buffet on the sideboard with cooked breakfast which I could help myself to. Just then Georgia arrived and ordered tea with toast and honey. She also asked for a glass of apple juice. I sat down again and asked John for a glass of orange juice. "I looked outside the window and saw that it was raining. "A miserable day." I said. "What again" exclaimed Georgia." I haven't watched the weather report but thought I could catch the news on TV" I said. Just then Alan appeared and greeted me asking if I had slept well. I told them about my briefcase and how I had awakened when I thought I had heard a noise in the room.

After checking my briefcase, I told them how the itineraries of some customers who had booked to go abroad had disappeared. It had the information about their flights and hotel accommodation. I don't know anybody who would want those papers. "Do you want us to call the Police?" asked Alan." No, it's not necessary. I have copies of the papers in my office in London. The matter was closed and momentarily I had the impression that everything was alright. Only time would tell if the theft was an important one.

CHAPTER 3

"Do you play Chess or Backgammon?" Georgia asked me. "I play both" I replied.

"That is excellent. You and Alan can play Chess this morning, and have a game of Backgammon with me this afternoon. It is raining and there isn't much for us to do today." said Georgia.

I suddenly remembered that they had a dog called Treff. I asked Georgia where he was.

Georgia replied that their dog had died last September of natural causes. He was an old dog. They weren't considering getting another dog for the time being.

Alan was about 60years, and Georgia was in her mid 50s. They were both in a good state of health playing golf at the Club and having a game of tennis in the summertime.

In the summer, when Jane and Gary came to stay a few days, they usually went swimming in their outdoor pool. They had not been down to the Manor for several months preferring to stay in their house in Wimbledon which they were busy doing up.

But they had accepted the invitation to Sunday's lunch party and would spend the day at the Manor. I had met them at their wedding and once afterwards at a party in Wandsworth, but I hadn't seen or heard from them since. I was delighted that we would be meeting again tomorrow at the party.

After viewing the news on TV Georgia turned it off and got up out of her chair and made her way out of the room towards the stairs leading up to her bedroom. I followed her. I returned to my own room. At about 10, I went downstairs again and sat in the Drawing Room with a newspaper which I slowly went through.

Alan came in shortly and proceeded to set up the games table for the game of chess. I drew up two chairs. I looked at the window and saw rain beating on the window pane.

John had made a nice warming fire. Alan and I sat down on the chairs and set about playing Chess for about an hour. Alan won.

After lunch, the weather had got colder and Georgia went up to the bedroom for her rest. Alan stayed on in the Drawing Room and kept me company. He eventually retired to the Study. I went upstairs to my room with a book in hand. I whiled away my time that afternoon stuck in a book about Modern Day Japan.

At about 4pm, there was a knock on my door. I opened the door and Georgia greeted me thanking me for waiting for her. We both went downstairs and sat at the same games table as in the morning. Georgia went to fetch the Backgammon set in the Study. She set it up prepared to play. We played for about an hour. I won. Georgia got up and tidied the table and the Backgammon set. She wanted to go to her room to get ready for the evening. She would change for dinner. I asked her if I could watch the News on TV. We parted our ways as the evening showed a darker sky.

CHAPTER 4

The next day turned out to be a lovely warm Spring day. The sun was shining and the world looked a different place then it had looked yesterday.

After breakfast, I stepped out of the house and walked on the gravel leading up to the house. It was still cold this morning but the weather would warm up later on. I had on my anorak. I walked a little further up an incline to the woods. One car passed me and the driver waved in a friendly manner. The ground was a little muddy but it was drying up.

John the butler was busy preparing the table in the covered terrace. The kitchen was busy, the cook preparing the lamb that we would eat for lunch. Georgia had extra help in to serve at the table.

By the time I got back from my walk, it was 12.30. I walked across to the terrace and found most of the guests had already arrived. John offered me champagne. I took a glass and sipped it. The first to greet me was Theresa. We talked a little while. I saw Jane and Gary. Theresa and I went over to them. They were talking to a tall blond lady. They introduced her to me. She was Princess Sophie Holenhoff of Bavaria, who nodded to us as she said "delighted to meet you." She continued her conversation with Jane and Gary. We moved on to see Alan who was having a lively conversation with Geraldine and Edward Hilley. Geraldine was an American lady living in London for many years. She was a millionairess and didn't work. She was involved with drugs and knew many in the London underworld. Edward Hilley, her companion was an old friend about the same age who worked at an American Bank in the city. In the meanwhile Georgia had returned fom the kitchen where the cook was preparing a large leg of lamb Lebanese style. She bade us all sit at the table. Name cards indicated where each person must sit. Suddenly a late arrival showed up. He was Martin Somerset an SAS officer who had seen a lot of action in Afghanistan. He was a tall handsome man with grey hair and sharp blue eyes. He made his apologies to Georgia and Alan. They welcomed him and said "Now come and sit down next to Princess Sophie. I think you have already met. They acknowledged each other as Martin kissed her hand, before sitting down.

There was talk of war in the Middle East that lunch time and the guests all turned to Martin who said "yes, I will probably be going to Syria. My men are ready and waiting for the command to leave."

The conversation became lively as they ate their lunch. Geraldine enjoyed the wine and drank excessively until she collapsed at the table her head falling onto the table mat. Edward Hilley was in a serious talk with Princess Sophie about stocks and shares. She agreed she had lost money and Edward was agreeable to explaining to her how the loss had occurred. Theresa and Gary talked of their respective properties and the work both were carrying out on them.

It was already 4pm when they got up from the table. The ladies went to the powder room while John served out liqueurs to the men. There were various settees and chairs in cane strewn around the terrace. When the women came back, they were offered a seat. Princess Sophie looked at her watch and started saying her goodbyes to the guests. She thanked Alan and Georgia for the marvellous lunch and company and made her way out of the grounds to the waiting car. Martin said his goodbyes to Georgia and Alan and to the other guests who remained. He walked over to the stone steps that would lead him to the front of the house where he had parked his car. Geraldine had collapsed on the cane chair and Edward was trying to revive her. Eventually she came to and staggering up, leaning on Edward's arm took small steps to Georgia and Alan. Thank you for a wonderful afternoon she slurred, as she stood unsteadily on her feet. Edward made his apologies and thanking the host and hostess left for his car parked near the front door. Finally Theresa went up to Alan and Georgia and said "what a great time I had today. Thank you for a wonderful lunch." She gave both of them a kiss on the cheek before she said goodbye to Kevin "hope to see you soon in London" she said to him. She made a hasty retreat back to her car..Jane and Gary had a long drive ahead of them and they would be leaving. They thanked John and said their goodbyes to their parents. "When we've finished work in the house you must come to us for a change and spend a week-end with us". "Oh, that would be splendid" said Alan. "We would love that." Jane gave her Mother and Father a hug and a kiss. Gary gave Alan a handshake and gave Georgia a kiss on the cheek. They made their way up the stone steps and disappeared from view as they went to their car to make their way back to Wimbledon.

There was only me left. Before I left, we sat for a while in silence by the terrace.

Georgia had ordered tea. When it arrived, John served the hot tea out and we gratefully drank it. "I must be leaving myself for London" I said. Tomorrow I must return to work. It's been a fun time spending the week-end here. I've really enjoyed myself and today's lunch was a great success. I sat next to your daughter Jane. She told me all about the improvements to their home and invited me over once the workmen had left. As I rose, they both got up and I shook

Alan's hand and gave Georgia a kiss on the cheek thanking her for the brilliant Lebanese lunch and wonderful wine. I went back to the house to fetch my case which was already packed. I checked the room first before leaving. I took the case and my anorak down stairs and out the front door It was now 5.30pm. I guessed I would be in London at about 7.

CHAPTER 5

"They'll get me in London, they won't try in the country" thought Pat to herself sitting in her armchair in her room. Max her husband had warned her about it a few years ago before his death. Now Pat was alone. I'll phone for a body guard, she thought, and make my way back to London. I'll leave tomorrow.

Pat was a widow. She was 60 years. She and Max had bought the country house in Gloucestershire about ten years ago. It was a four bedroom house. There was a garden and land attached to the house. Pat had a housekeeper called Madeline who came in everyday to clean, shop and cook. She had a son called Karl who went to school in the local village. Her husband worked in an office usually in front of a computer. He worked for transportation. Madeline had worked for the Walters ever since they had moved in.

She knocked on Pat's bedroom door. She heard a voice saying "come in". She opened the door and found Pat busily packing her suitcase. This came as a surprise to Madeline." Can I help you?" she asked. "Yes, please fetch my blue dress and my black evening dress out of the closet and my black evening shoes. I need my silk shawl".

"Will you be gone for long?" asked Madeline. "Indefinitely" said Pat." I have some business to attend to in London. I'll let you know if I will be longer than one week. I want you to come in every other day to keep an eye on the house and see to it that the house is clean and that nothing goes missing."

Pat had a flat off Grosvenor Square in South Audley Street. She decided to take a car service to London and leave her own car in the garage in the country.

She phoned Brown's body guard agency and applied for a bodyguard the next day at the flat. She knew it would be expensive. She then phoned Allen & Hawkes solicitors and made an appointment to see Jeremy Henderson the family solicitor at 10.30am the next day. She then phoned her son Bill but there was no reply. Pat left a phone message for him. She told him she was temporarily moving back to the flat in London.

The doorbell went half an hour later. It was the car service. Madeline opened the door and let the driver in to take the luggage and put it in the boot of the car. Pat put on her coat and stepped outside saying her goodbye to Madeline. Soon she would be in London.

CHAPTER 6

The next day, with Chuck the bodyguard, Pat walked into the offices of Allen and

Hawkes. She didn't have to wait long to see her solicitor Jeremy Henderson. He greeted her warmly and pointed at the chair for her to sit down on. After enquiring politely about herself and her family, he said "what can I do for you today?" She replied sadly that Geraldine Price was giving her a problem. She wanted the sum of £10million from her for a loan of money she had given Max years ago before he died. He had borrowed £12million but because Geraldine and the Walters were old friends Geraldine would accept less and demanded repayment of £10million. If this could not be agreed, then Pat may have to go. Jeremy, knew well enough that Geraldine Price was a drug dealer and drug addict. He realized that Pat was being badly threatened. He told Pat to pay her back as quickly as possible if she had the money. Pat had the money but hesitated paying her back. She knew Geraldine might come back to her for more money in a year or two. This was the reason for her visit to see Jeremy. She asked Jeremy to take it to Court so that the hand-over was legally bound. She asked Jeremy if Geraldine could legally come back to her for more without it looking like black-mail. Jeremy told her he would help her as far as the Court case went. He would tell the barrister about her concerns of black-mail and possible further payment demands to Geraldine. This could happen anytime. "Yes" he said," taking this to Court is a very good idea. I will arrange and let you know by e-mail when we will meet again". He added, "I see you came with a companion". "He's my bodyguard for a few days said Pat. He's not cheap" she added. After a few minutes, Pat got up from her chair and thanked Jeremy for seeing her so quickly. She realised he usually had a busy schedule. They said their goodbyes and Pat left the office. Chuck saw her and got up to greet her. They both left the Reception area and went outdoors where he hailed down a black taxi to take them to a Japanese restaurant in Dover Street. They both enjoyed drinking Japanese sake or rice wine and ordered a fine lunch. It had been a long time since Pat had been out to a restaurant. She particularly enjoyed eating Japanese food. After lunch Pat went to the hairdresser and had her hair trimmed and blow-dryed. Her hair-dresser Nick was pleased to see her. He offered her a glass of French champagne which she accepted. The body guard was waiting for her at the Reception where there was a sofa and an armchair. After paying Nick a tip Pat paid the bill of £75. Everything in London had gone up in price she noticed. She put on her coat at the coat check in and returned to Chuck who was busy looking at a magazine. When he saw her, he got up and together they walked to the door which he held open for her. Her flat was within walking distance. They walked back to the flat that sunny and warm afternoon.

When they reached the flat, she asked Chuck to check the windows, doors and rooms. He even checked the TV. She had taken off her coat. It was now 4.10 in the afternoon. She thanked Chuck and said she would see him tomorrow morning at 11. He then said "Is that all?" She nodded in response. He then took his leave closing the flat door behind him.

CHAPTER 7

Bill was in the army. He was stationed at a camp near Winchester. He had seen action in Afghanistan. He had been back for two weeks and was about to go back to Winchester. His wife Penny was there with their two year old son Daniel. He could take a one month leave before returning to Kabul. Penny wanted him to retire from active duty because of her fear for his life fighting the Taliban. Bill wanted to stay on. He was on his way back home today, and before he left he gave his Mother a phone call.

"Hello Mummy. This is Bill" he said." "Oh, I want to see you. It's been ages since we last met" she said. "How are all of you? Keeping well I expect. It's been over six months since our last meeting." After catching up on each other's news, Pat said, "Can you and Penny come up to London to have lunch with me next week?" "Oh that would be wonderful", said Bill." I'm sure Penny would love that." "Well then, that's settled" said Pat." Meet me at Gerards as usual in Piccadilly at 12.30 next Tuesday. I'm sure this will be good for Penny", she said thoughtfully. "I'll confirm this with you later when I get a chance to see Penny to ask her. Otherwise, how have you been keeping?" asked Bill?

"Oh. I'm in good health. I have so far no medical problems," she continued.

Just then, Captain Saunders interrupted their talk to tell Bill that the bus was waiting for him. Bill said his hasty goodbye to his Mother, and told her he would be back in touch with her later on that day, once he had spoken to Penny about next Tuesday.

He then picked up his bags and walked briskly to the exit

door and went to the waiting bus and got in.. The bus jolted forward and left the stop.

An hour later, he was in front of his house in Winchester. He opened the door and greeted his wife Penny." Hello, I'm home" he yelled. His wife came running in to him with open arms and gave him a great big hug and kiss." I'm so glad to see you she said. You've lost weight and you're very sun tanned. Come, take your cases to the bedroom. I'm just preparing lunch for the two of us. Daniel is having a rest. He's not due to get up for another hour. Oh, it's good to see you. I've missed you", she exclaimed. They caught up on each other's news over lunch.

After lunch, Bill helped his wife in the kitchen. He helped her clear the table and put the plates and cutlery into the dishwasher. When this was done, he went to their room and unpacked. He lay down on the bed for a rest and dozed off. When he awakened, he was shocked to see that it was already 5pm. He slowly got up and made his way downstairs to find Penny. She wasn't there. A note was left on the kitchen table which read "Gone out to do some shopping. Back soon, Penny."

He sat down on the sofa and turned on the TV to watch the news.

About a quarter of an hour later Penny came in with Daniel. She had a lot of groceries. Bill helped her with the shopping bags. It had been a long time since he helped with the housekeeping." Did you phone the babysitter?" asked Bill. Penny rang Mrs Mckenzie the babysitter and asked her if she could baby sit for part of a day looking after Daniel next Tuesday.." How is my Daniel?" she asked. "Oh, he's very well said Penny" ".Well, I look forward to seeing you all at 11 next Tuesday the 27th. Nice speaking to you" she said. She put her phone down.

Bill took Daniel out of his pushchair and took him in his arms and held him close. He kissed him and talked to him. Daniel had grown and was a regular little toddler. The happiness on Bill's face was all too apparent what the child meant to him.

Daniel would be attending the Montessori school in the autumn. In the meanwhile Penny would prepare his tea and after that, let him play after which he would have a bath before preparing for sleep in his cot. After this, Bill and Penny would have a drink before preparing dinner for themselves. The sun was setting and it was a warm cloudless evening. Just before sitting down, Bill opened a bottle of white wine and lit the candles on the dining table in the kitchen. Bill would reminisce about his days and nights in Afghanistan and tell Penny about his best friend David who had died in action. The Taliban got him. The evening lingered on and soon it was 9pm, time to clear up the table and get on with the washing up. When they had finished clearing up, they crept up the stairs and went into the bedroom. There Bill took Penny in his arms and gave her a long lingering kiss. The night would bring them love and passion that most lovers have after an absence. They would both awake at the dawn of another beautiful warm day.

At 12.30 on Tuesday, they met Pat who was already seated at the table of Gerards restaurant. Bill greeted her with a kiss on the cheek. Both he and Penny took their seats around the table. The menu was brought to them. The waiter asked them if they would like a drink. They ordered a glass each of French champagne to celebrate their re-union.

They looked at the menu. Pat ordered fish and Penny

ordered a London mixed grill while Bill opted for a rib eye steak. After their order Pat explained that it was an old bill. The family solicitor was engaged in legalising the transfer from Pat's account to Geraldine's account. Pat explained that it was an old debt that Dad had borrowed from Geraldine some twenty years before. Pat also told them that she had hired a body guard from Brown's security. "Will you be returning to the country after the payment has been settled?" asked Penny. I think so if all goes well tomorrow. said Pat.

They ate their lunch. Penny had nothing but praise for the cook of the restaurant and told Pat what a treat it was to be taken there today.

Turning to Bill, Pat asked" how long is your leave this time?" "About a month. I expect to leave for Kabul on the 5th of September for an indefinite period of time". He told her about David his best friend who had got killed in action." They had done everything to save him at the hospital but he never pulled through. His body was transported to the UK and his family buried him in the country cemetery near his home in Devon. It was a great loss for me," he said thoughtfully.

When they had finished lunch, Pat asked for the bill and when it came paid for it by card. They all three got up and made their way out of the restaurant.. It had been a nice day.. Bill hailed down a taxi which drove them to the flat in South Audley street. It was now 4pm. They accompanied Pat into her flat and settled her in; They stayed only a few minutes before leaving for the station to go back to Winchester. Bill wondered when he would see his Mother again while he was on leave. Perhaps they would visit her at home in Gloucestershire for a weekend with Daniel he thought to himself. He would speak to her sometime in the week and suggest this to her. He thought that his Mother looked well and fit and five years younger. Country life obviously suited her. He looked forward to hearing about the transfer of money and knew that with Jeremy Henderson, she would pull through successfully. It was all for tomorrow when the family debt of £10million would be paid.

CHAPTER 8

The next day Pat sat at the office of Jeremy Henderson. She signed the paper that would pay the money over to Geraldine. Jeremy counter signed it. This took only a few minutes.

"Well, that is done" said Jeremy. "She will have the money by the end of the week. Is there anything else I can help you with?" he asked.

"That is all for the time being. Let us hope Max had no other debt." she said. She got up from the chair and shook Jeremy's hand.. "Thank you" she said to him. She turned to go to the door and Jeremy opened the door for her and let her out. Her bodyguard got up when she came out to the Reception area and together they made their way out of the building They walked out into the street where Chuck hailed down a taxi. They made their way to Harry's Bar where they would eat lunch. Pat told Chuck over lunch that she would not be requiring his services after- to day, that she would be returning to the country.

When they had finished lunch, Chuck walked Pat back to her flat. It was a pleasant and mild afternoon with a sunny sky. Once arrived they made their way to the second floor flat where Pat turned the key to her flat and they both walked in. Chuck said his goodbye to Pat after checking the flat again and securing the windows. She asked that one of the windows remained open on that warm day. He left leaving her to think about Geraldine and also wondering if there were other debts that would have to be. settled. She sat on the sofa and eventually dozed off. She woke up an hour later and looked at her watch. It was 5pm. She got up slowly and made her way to the bedroom. She opened her suitcase and started putting some of her clothes in it. Tomorrow she would be back in the country and glad to be home. She had lost a lot of money but she knew that for the time being all was well.

The next morning at 11, the buzzer went on the intercom. It was Jack the driver, sent from the country to pick her up to take her back home to Gloucestershire. Her bags were packed and she was ready to leave. Jack came up and took the case from her flat. Before leaving, she closed the open window and locked it. She set the alarm and left the flat. As she opened the door to step outside, she felt a sharp pain on her left leg. She looked down at her leg and saw a scratch mark on it. She thought it was nothing significant. She walked to the car and Jack opened the car door for her. She jumped inside. She put her coat next to her in the adjoining sea and put her seat belt on. Jack drove the car and made his way out of the West End and hit the motorway. While in the car, Pat experienced drowsiness and kept falling asleep. She slept for most of the journey. Jack had to awaken her when they arrived in front of her house.

Jack took the suitcase out of the boot of the car and put the case in front of the door. He opened the car door to let Pat out. Pat got out slowly and told Jack she had been shot when she came out into the street to get in the car. Jack immediately asked her if he could phone for her doctor. She managed to open the front door of her house and together they went in. . She went into the drawing room and collapsed into a chair. Jack followed her. She phoned the surgery and told the Receptionist that she had been shot outside her flat in London. She had to see the doctor today as she felt drowsy and weak. The Reception told her to come to the surgery as soon as possible.

The surgery was in Hamwell Place. He helped her out of the chair and led her to the car. Once in the car Jack drove her to Hamwell Place. He helped her out of the car and helped her walk a short distance to the surgery. The Receptionist who was expecting her told her to sit in the waiting room. She would be the next person to see the doctor. She asked Jack to wait for her. He sat next to her in the waiting room. She was called in after ten minutes. She staggered to his room and immediately sat down on the chair opposite his desk. She stammered as she told him what had happened to her outside her flat in the street. Doctor Simpson looked at her left leg and saw a swelling on it.

He took Pat's temperature and saw she had a high fever. He felt her pulse and checked her blood pressure which was high. He told her she had to go into hospital. He rang the hospital and talked to admissions and reserved a bed for her. He told her to go there right away. The doctor let her lean on him as he walked her out of his room. Jack got up when he saw them and the doctor having asked him if he was her driver. Dr. Simpson told him to take her to admissions in St. Claire's hospital . They were expecting her. He led Pat to the car and once in, he drove quickly to the hospital where he checked her in at admissions. Once the nurse was in charge, he took leave of her and watched her being wheel chaired to her room. He left rather sadly and drove back to the office.

Once in her room, they helped her take off her clothes and put the hospital gown on. A nurse came in to take a blood test and inspect the leg. The doctor eventually came into the room, but by then, Pat had fallen asleep. He would pass by later on. The nurse told the doctor what Pat had told her. He looked carefully at the leg. There was an abrasion. The blood test would tell him what they shot into her. Her GP Dr Simpson talked to Dr Kelly on the telephone and told him she had a temperature of 101 and that her blood pressure was high. Dr Kelly was grateful for the call. At 6pm, Dr Kelly went back to see Pat who was propped up in bed with a jug of water. Chatting Pat up, he got a few answers from her of how she had got shot. The results of the blood test would be out by the next morning. He told her he would see her again in the morning and took his leave to see his other patients on the ward.

By 7pm Pat was soundly asleep. The nurse left her and put the night light on in her room and turned off the main lights. There were periodic checks on her throughout the night by the nurse in attendance. This continued until the next morning.

When she woke up, Pat only wanted water to drink. The doctor showed up at 9.30 and told her the results of the blood test. She had yellow fever, a tropical disease, not usually found in England. He put her on medicine and told her she would soon feel more herself. The nurse came in with medicine for her to swallow. By 12noon, Pat was feeling improved though weak. She slept.

It would be two months before she could go home. She had never been so badly upset by bad health as now. She would know in a month or two who had shot her and why.

Until then she was under the care of nurses and doctor. She fell asleep again.

CHAPTER 9

Kevin was at his desk at the travel agency when he received a phone call from the Police. They enquired about two passengers from Nairobi called Theodore Gusmann and Matthew Steigle. They had flown in over the week-end of last week and had brought in a lot of drugs in their cases. The Police believed they were drug traffickers. Their present whereabouts were unknown. Kevin told the Police that he would check up on them. He told them he had a contact in Nairobi who would be able to help identify the two white men. He took a note of the Police telephone number and the name of the policeman in charge of the investigation. He asked the police to give him one whole day to find out about them, and he would phone in a couple of days and tell them what he knew.

In the afternoon, he e-mailed Stanley Asner, a tour operator, and told him about his problem. He told Stanley to e-mail him back with any information he could find about them. Kevin got back a reply from Stanley who asked him to wait a day or two for his brief.

In the meanwhile, Kevin checked the flights of an English businessman on his way to Dubai to meet leaders of oil production in that country. Another air-flight ticket had been reserved for a Mr. and Mrs. Finn who were on their way to Hawaii to visit their daughter and son-in-law. A third air-ticket had been issued for a Father Doughty who was travelling to Rome. Then he looked over the air-ticket of Count and Countess de Villeneuve who were off to Biarritz for a long week-end. They were all flying British Airways. They would be travelling within the next two weeks. He double checked each air-ticket and it all appeared to be valid and good. He often wondered why the original itinerary had been stolen from his room at the Manor House. It was a mysterious theft. He sent off the tickets that day and posted them.

A day passed without any news from Stanley in Nairobi. Then the following day Kevin received an e-mail from him in the afternoon. It read:

Theodore Gusman and Matthew Steigle both nurses at the Nairobi Central Hospital.

Both deal with tropical medicine. Gusman had worked there for ten years. Steigle had worked there for six years. There had been an incident last week in South Audley street, London, Mayfair, when a Mrs Pat Avery-Smith was shot in the leg with an agent of yellow fever. She saw her country doctor in Gloucestershire that afternoon and was rushed to hospital. Now in a ward in the Princess Margaret hospital she is recovering from the attack. It is believed Gusmann shot her. They want money. Rs Avery-Smith had just paid a debt to a Gerladine Price, a drug dealer. Mrs. Avery-Smith's husband had borrowed £10million from her many years before, and had never paid back the debt. Now it has been settled Gusman and Steigle threatened Pat and wanted payment of £10million from her. They have never met.

Please send a copy of this e-mail to the police. Vital they receive this report.

So long,

Stanley

Kevin looked at his watch and saw that it had gone past 5pm. He quickly got on his computer and sent off a copy of Stanley's e-mail to the CID Officer a Mark Galbraith at Scotland Yard.

He sent them a note which he signed so that they would know who sent it. In a few minutes he received an e-mail from them acknowledging receipt of the e-mail from Stanley.

In Nairobi as night set, Stanley was ready to leave the café where he had eaten dinner. Suddenly the waiter shouted at Stanley to get down. Stanley lay on the ground for a few moments and the knife attacker ran into the street brandishing a large knife and was lost to the world as he disappeared into the night. He was wearing a kerchief to cover his face. Stanley got up from the ground as the Nairobi Police arrived.

They got an account of what had happened by Stanley and the clients of the café, who were witnesses to the attempted murder. The waiter was the star witness. His evidence was the most realistic. When the Police left, Stanley stayed at the pavement of the café at a table and ordered a brandy which he gulped down quickly. When his composure had come back, he went up to the waiter and thanked him for saving his life. Before he went home he gave the waiter a tip. He walked back. Once back in his flat, he put on the air conditioner and closed and locked all the doors and windows. There was so far no sign of the knife attacker. He turned off the light in the sitting room and went to his bedroom. He checked the bathroom. He changed into his pyjamas and after brushing his teeth and wetting his face, he went to bed turning off all the lights except the night light. He went to bed and fell asleep. At about 2.30 in the morning he suddenly woke up aware of a presence either in the flat or outside the front door. He got out of bed and opened the bedside drawer pulling out a gun.

He put on his dressing gown and slippers and went to the door. He could hear the prowler in the sitting room. He decided not to open the bedroom door for that would only make things worse for him. He decided to sit on his chair with no lights on and wait there to see what would happen. The prowler eventually came to the door of the bedroom. He silently turned the knob of the door which was locked. He tried to force the door open without keys. Stanley prepared himself for a shoot out. He got his gun ready to fire. The prowler could be the knife attacker. Stanley was certain there was a connection. Suddenly the door burst open and shots were fired. The prowler slumped to the floor blood pouring from his chest. Stanley phoned the Police and asked for an ambulance. He turned on the lights. A quarter of an hour later, the Police and ambulance arrived. They entered Stanley's flat and saw the body of the prowler on the floor covered in blood. The paramedics leaned down over him and saw that he was still just alive. They got the stretcher and put the body of the prowler on it.

They left for the hospital. The Police got a report from Stanley who showed them his gun. They did not need him to come down to the Police Station for the time being.

They only told him not to leave the country for a month. They were going to the hospital to find out who the man was who Stanley shot. Before they left, they asked Stanley to lock all the doors and windows. Stanley was alone in his flat by 4.30. He turned off the lights again after locking up. He suddenly felt tired. He never told the Police about the case of the two medical nurses in London. He knew his e-mail to

Kevin had upset someone very badly, so badly they sent a

hired killer to him twice that night to get rid of him. In spite of what had happened Stanley slept relatively peacefully and got up in the morning to go to work as usual/ "What a night!" he thought to himself.

CHAPTER 10

It had been a month since Kevin last heard from Stanley. He wondered if the Police case was going well. He had heard that they had caught Theodore Gusmann and Matthew Steigle. They were both awaiting a sentence. It looked like they were going to be deported back to Kenya, where they would face a trail.

Kevin had dispatched all the flight tickets to the passengers who were going off to various European destinations. Father Doughty would be the first to fly to Rome.

His flight would take off tomorrow at 10. Mr. and Mrs Finn were due to take off for Honolulu at 5pm tomorrow. The businessman, a Lionel Fitzroy was due to depart tomorrow at 12noon. The French couple would be flying off for Biarritz at 2pm, the day after tomorrow. When it was Father's Doughty's turn to leave, nobody would have suspected that anything could go wrong. But as the day wore on, the flight never landed at Rome airport. Air flight control had lost contact with the aircraft. The plane had disappeared. Kevin got in touch with the diocese where the priest lived. He told them what had happened and assured them hat he would keep them updated. with further news

The media swept in and got a full report from the civil aviation authority. It was on the early evening news.

There were 80 people on board the Rome flight. Some were British tourists, the other, Italians returning home. British Airways had to find telephone numbers and names of the closest relatives to notify them of the mishap. At Rome airport, they were busy with Italian airport management to try to locate the missing aircraft. It was early days. Maybe they would find it eventually but it didn't look good right now.

Kevin wondered if the lost air ticket itinerary that had gone missing from his Briefcase the week-end he spent with the Gibsons could have been connected to the relevant disappearance of the airplane. He eventually got around to telling the Police at the airport about the theft. It might help them with the case.

"Was there anybody important on board the airplane?" asked Theresa when Kevin met up with her at a party Prada was giving. "I haven't looked at the list" said Kevin. But it's not impossible that there was a VIP on board returning home. I'll check it out" he said.

Kevin and Theresa stayed a little longer at the party sipping champagne. Theresa was with one of her clients who tried on a pair of sandals. She liked them enough to buy them. Theresa led her to the cash desk and after paying heavily for the sandals left the shop thanking Theresa for her help. Theresa then went back to Kevin. It was now 8.30 and Theresa went up to the floor manager to ask if she could leave to have dinner with a friend. As there was just a dwindling amount of customers left in the shop, the Manager a Mr Ford-Thompson told her she could go. "Thank you" she said to him and went to pick up her umbrella and coat and handbag and returned to Kevin, who was waiting for her. Kevin took her to Chelsea where they entered a well known restaurant which was busy and very lively.

They stayed at the restaurant until 10.30. Kevin and Theresa got into a black taxi, and made their way first to Draycott Avenue to drop Theresa off, then onto Ebury Street to Kevin's pad. They both had to work the next day and it was getting late. It had been a fun evening, and Kevin and

Theresa were getting o know each other better.

As Kevin entered his flat, he heard the phone ringing. He opened the door quickly and switched on a light. He went to pick up the phone in the living room It was a call from the British tour operator's office. A voice explained that it was very important.

Stanley had been killed in Nairobi. A marksman had got him/ Stanley was dead.

Asking the tour operator whose name was Bryan, what time Stanley had been killed, he was told , it was about 12.30 in the afternoon when he stepped out of the office to have a coffee. The Police found the marksman and he was arrested and taken to the police station. Kevin asked him if Stanley's body has been claimed by his closest relatives. He was told they had been notified and arrangements would be made for a burial.

"I'd like to attend the funeral" said Kevin to Bryan." Let me know when it will take place and where it will be held. "It's late" said Bryan. But we'll talk tomorrow. "

"Bye for now" as he put his phone down. Kevin was shocked by the news. He sat down in the armchair of his living room and thought hard about Stanley and the circumstances that led to his brutal death He could hardly believe it. He stayed up late and fell asleep in the chair.. When he awakened it was already 6.30 in the morning. "I won't go to bed now "he thought to himself as he wearily got up. It would take time to settle back to his routine and his life. But he was young and the future was his.

CHAPTER 11

After Stanley's burial, there was a party and Kevin was introduced to his family. The Asners were average Middle Class white people. Mrs Asner was overcome by grief but controlled this and was able to hold a conversation with Kevin. Stanley's younger sister Dorothy was a student at London University studying medicine. She wanted to become a doctor, a GP. She would surely miss her brother. Then there were various relatives and friends who attended the party. Kevin managed to say hello to all of them. The party finished at 6pm. Kevin came out of the hotel after saying goodbye to everybody and went back to his hotel, Hotel Montressa. Tomorrow he would be on the flight home. He would have to re-open his suitcase and be ready to leave the hotel at 12noon.

After paying his bill, Kevin went to the bar of the hotel and ordered a coca cola. When he had finished, he got up and made his way to the front door of the hotel. The doorman whistled for a taxi that were lined up near the front door. Kevin got in while his case was put in the boot of the taxi. The taxi switched on the metre and drove to the airport. Once there, Kevin paid the taxi driver and got out of the taxi. He made his way to the BA counter and checked in handing in his case. The airport was air conditioned that hot September afternoon.

He decided to have something to eat at one of the restaurants. He saw one which looked clean and tidy. He read the menu and ordered a club sandwich and a beer.

Shortly after finishing his lunch, he paid the bill and made his way to the screen. Yes the gate was open and he walked to gate number 6 for Heathrow.

The plane journey went without incident and he arrived at Heathrow airport 3 hours later. He went through passport control and immigration without a problem and went to wait for a black taxi to take him back home.

Two days later, Kevin received a phone call from Airport Security telling him that flight BA 304 to Rome had not yet been found. It had flown through Italian territory but disappeared as it approached Rome. There was a Cardinal Brennan on board the aircraft sitting in First Class. There was to be a meeting of the Cardinals in the Vatican. Father Doughty was a part of the meeting. He was travelling economy class.

There was no more information. Radar had lost sight of the airplane. The plane was lost. Kevin would have to answer to all the friends and relatives of the passengers on board the flight. He had a big task in front of him.

CHAPTER 12

Jane and Gary had finished putting in their new Conservatory and painting the house both outside and inside. Jane's parents Alan and Georgia Gibson would be arriving in the afternoon to spend a week-end with them.

Tonight they planned to go to a Japanese restaurant specializing in Teppanyaki where the cook prepares the meat and fish in front of you on the electric grill. Alan had eaten Japanse food before but it would be the first time for Georgia. Gary busied himself with the bar and put white and rose wine in the fridge. He also put in a bottle of French champagne.

Shortly it had turned 4:30, which was the time they were expected to arrive from the country. John would be keeping an eye on the house while they were away. Finally, at 4:45, the doorbell rang. They had arrived. Gary opened the door and helped his in- laws with the luggage.. When Alan came into the house discussing the parking situation, Alan was told to park his car on a yellow line knowing he would not get a ticket. It was the weekend. Jane was busy talking to her Mother. When Alan came into the house Jane showed them upstairs with Gary who was carrying the cases. The room was on the second floor, beautifully furnished with antique furniture they received when they married. The room had first class views of the garden below.

Jane asked her parents if they'd like tea after their long journey. Their seats at the Miyako restaurant was reserved for 7.30 that evening. Both Georgia and Alan thought they would like a bottle of mineral water which Georgia spotted on the side table next to the bed. She wanted time for a bath before changing for dinner. She needed time to unpack.

Jane showed her parents the ensuite bathroom and shower.

Afterwards Jane and Gary retired to the kitchen downstairs where Jane had been preparing canapes for drinks. She had even gone to the expense of buying a small pot of Iranian caviar. She would put the cavier on some small blinis. She had also bought some Scottish smoked salmon and put the salmon in twirls on small pieces of bread.

When she was done, she put the plate of canapés into the fridge. She went upstairs and joined her husband in the bedroom. Tonight she would wear her silk Prada dress. She took a shower and got ready to change. Gary was already changed and was putting on his shoes." I think I'll open the bottle of champagne" he said to his wife. "Sounds good to me" said Jane.

By the time Jane had changed and put on her make up, it was already 6pm. Gary went upstairs and knocked on the visitor's door and told them that drinks were ready. Georgia was lying on top of the bed fully dressed. Alan thanked Gary and after Georgia had got up, they both made their way down to the kitchen to find that drinks with canapés were ready "How perfectly splendid" exclaimed Alan. There was a lovely bottle of champagne in a wine cooler and wonderful looking canapés. Jane led them into the drawing room with the plate full of canapés held in her hand.

After drinks they made their way to the Miyako Restaurant. Alan was delighted at being taken to a Japanese restaurant and Georgia was excited at the thought of eating Japanese food.

Once arrived at the restaurant in Wimbledon,, they were seated at the counter where the chef arrived and made a bow to them introducing himself. It was a wonderful evening. Alan had fillet steak and lobster, Georgia ordered chicken and prawn. Gary ordered fillet steak and prawn. Alan and Georgia marvelled at the way the chef used his knife to cut the meat and the fish. Otherwise it was delicious and a lot of fun to eat. They ate their meal with rice cooked on the grill.

When it came time to pay the bill, Gary carried it off beautifully and paid the bill. It included several bottles of sake or rice wine and mineral water. Alan tried to intercede but was abruptly turned away by Gary.

They all four left the restaurant contented and happy. The evening had been a surprise party for Alan and Georgia.

The week-end had gone well with walks and sightseeing. Their sightseeing included walks on Wimbledon Common and a visit to a museum of arts and crafts.

On Sunday, they had been invited to Sunday lunch by Steven and his brother Gregory who worked in the same law office Wellby and Hamilton.

After their coffee, Alan and Georgia got up and thanked their hosts for the lunch.

Gary and Jane also got up and said what a great lunch it had been.

They followed their parents to the front door. They all stepped out into a clear sunny day and made their way to the car. They got in the car and Gary turned on the engine and moved forward to the main road. Steven and Gregory waved goodbye to them and the four of them went off.

After returning back home, Alan and Georgia went to their room to finish off the packing and Alan took the two cases down the stairs with Georgia trailing behind him carrying their coats. Alan and Georgia gave Jane a big hug and kissed her cheek thanking her for a wonderful weekend. Alan shook Gary's hand thanking him and Georgia gave him a kiss on the cheek saying what a wonderful host he was. Alan took the cases to the car and deposited them in the boot of the car. They climbed into their car and went off waving goodbye to Jane and Gary who were standing by the front door waving to them.

CHAPTER 13

BA flight 304 had lost radar control. The pilot had no idea where he was except that they were in the middle of a desert far away from Rome airport. He tried to put on the telephone and radio but nothing worked. The plane had crash landed and there was nothing but desert all around with not a soul in sight. The crew gave a drink of water to all 80 passengers on board.

The co-pilot got out of the plane and sent a flame from a torch hoping somebody would see their sign for rescue. The pilot tried to make radio contact. It was 4pm Rome time. They had been there for two days. The food had run out and there was only water but even that was running out. Suddenly through the window of the plane, the pilot saw clouds of sand in the distance moving in their direction. He could not make out how many vehicles there were. Through the loudspeaker, the pilot a Mark Scott told the good news to the passengers. The passengers were all relieved to know that somebody else was in the desert and would probably find them.

At 6pm, the pilot and passengers saw a military vehicle approaching with soldiers in it. By 7pm they saw clearly both the vehicles and soldiers. They stopped by the BA plane and got out. The head of their troop got out first and indicated to one of the soldiers to speak in English to the pilots. The pilot got out of the airplane and met the soldiers. The pilot explained that the flight should have gone to Rome but they had lost radar and radio control. He was told they were in the Sinai desert far away from Rome. Then he was told buses would come to collect the passengers and crew the next morning. The buses would take them to Jerusalem.

He asked the pilot how many passengers were on board. When he heard that there were 80 passengers, 3crew plus two pilots, the Israeli soldier told him how lucky he was to have survived. After an hour, the soldiers left making their way out of the desert. It wouldn't be long before they were rescued. The passengers put their blankets over themselves and waited for the morning.

The next day as the sun was rising, the pilot saw the buses in the desert. The passengers were awakened and got ready to leave the airplane. When the buses arrived they parked themselves a short distance from the aircraft. The hatch was opened and the passengers slid down an emergency chute down to the bottom. There was no particular problem amongst the passengers and as they reached the bottom of the chute they got up and walked over to the waiting bus. This went on for an hour. As each bus filled up, they were driven away across the desert towards Jerusalem. Once at the airport they had to fill in a form stating name, nationality and address. They were given small bottles of water and told to sit in the waiting room. Later on in the morning, they were told they would be taken to the Hilton Hotel in town, where they would receive delivery of their luggage later on at the end of the day. The first to leave were the first class passengers. They boarded a bus which went off at lunchtime to the town centre and to the hotel. The rest of the passengers were called about an hour later and told buses would take them to the hotel where they would stay until arrangements were made to put them on board another BA flight to Rome.

A few hours later, they were settling into their rooms, many of the passengers made their way back to the lobby to go to the coffee shop where they could eat and drink. Others made their way to the bar. It had been a long four days for them and they were relieved and grateful to God for being delivered out of the desert and into Israel where the soldiers had taken them.

At 7pm, that evening, the passengers took delivery of their luggage. The porters busily assisted them with their luggage to their rooms. The delighted passengers could now change into their clothes and brush their teeth.

Tomorrow they would know when they could hope to get on board another flight to take them back to Europe and to Rome.

At Rome airport five days later, Cardinal Brennan and Father Doughty were met by Monsignor Octavio and whisked away out of the airport towards the Vatican. Both had missed the meeting that was to take place a week ago. Most of the delegates had already left. However they would meet Pope Luke 1V and apologise for their delay in arriving. I hear you got stranded in the Sinai desert said Pope Luke to Cardinal Brennan. "Why yes, we thought we were there for good" said Father Doughty. "It was a miracle that the Israeli military patrol saw us and the torch that was sent. God took care of us and His Guardian Angel made sure somebody would rescue us." said Cardinal Brennan. "It was a miracle" he repeated.

As they spoke of their adventure inside the aircraft in the middle of the desert, the Pope took them to his dining table and they sat down to lunch of pasta and fried zucchini. After finishing chocolate and mango ice cream they rose from the table and followed Pope Luke into the garden room. There they sat down and had their coffee. He continued the brief the Pope gave them about the meeting of the Cardinals. "It was agreed almost unanimously that the Church would not allow in women priests."

"There is a strong quota of women who want to be women priests in England" said Cardinal Brennan. I doubt the results of the meeting will be favourable to our parishioners." he added. "Well, I'm in favour of the meetings results" said Father Doughty. I cannot say I like the idea of women being treated for priests" he added.

It would make the Catholic Church comparable to the Church of England who have women priests." "The big difference between the two Churches is that the Anglican Church allow priests to be married. The Catholics are not permitted to marry. I wonder if one day soon, marriage of priests in the Church can be discussed with a view to allowing priests to marry. It would become a more blessed sacrament and there would be less cases of child sex abuse." said Cardinal Brennan.

"That is most interesting "said the Pope. "I will make a point of discussing this in our next meeting in six month's time. I could consider allowing marriage for the clergy."

After deliberating for a time, the Pope rose and said his goodbyes to both the Cardinal and the priest. He blessed them and took them to the door of the drawing room which led outside. Cardinal Brennan went first followed by Father Doughty. The two only had the day left in Rome before they took their flight the next day back to Heathrow. It had been an inspirational talk and one which they wrote down in their diary as a blessed one.

CHAPTER 14

Pat had been in the hospital for two months. She had made good recovery and was up and about on the ward. Soon she would be allowed to go back home. Bill and Penny had been to visit her a few times. Bill returned to Afghanistan leaving Penny and their two year old. Bill would see them again in about three months. Bill worried about his Mother's health and her inevitable return to the house. He tried to persuade her to have a carer look after her for a month or two but she was not taken by the idea. However she said "I'll consider what you say" When the time came for her to leave the hospital she had a carer pick her up to take her back home. She would keep the carer in her employ for about a month. The carer was a Mrs Fitzsimmons. She had a good reputation and was renowned for her good cooking and her wit. Some of Pat's friends had employed her and found her to be very good.

When Pat entered the house, she saw that everything was clean. When she looked out at the garden, she was horrified to see how overgrown it was. She knew she must phone the gardener and make an appointment with them. The lawn was overgrown, the grass high. The flower bed showed wilted and dead flowers. The hedges had become thick and over grown. "What a mess" she said aloud.

Mrs. Fitzsimmons helped her unpack. Afterwards, she went downstairs to make some tea. There were only two teabags left. Pat got out the notepad and pen from the drawer and put down tea on the shopping list. The maid had put in fresh milk in the fridge and there were biscuits. There was a packet of fresh salmon for tonight and some new potatoes and broccoli. She would ask Madeleine to pick up some tea on her way to work tomorrow.

After tea, Pat decided to have a rest in her room until drinks time at 6. It was now 4.30. Mrs Fitzsimmons had to clear up the kitchen and set the table for dinner in the kitchen. Before going up, Pat showed her how to work the television and radio. After this, she went up for her rest. Mrs Fitzsimmons decided to take a walk after she had finished her chores. It was a sunny afternoon and a perfect day for a walk.

When the clock struck 6, Pat came down the stairs. She wore the same thing she had worn in the daytime. She helped herself to a glass of white wine and made her way to the sofa to watch the evening News. Mrs Fitzsimmons had returned from her walk.

Both ladies sat on the large sofa and watched the news. Mrs Fitzsimmons enquired how Pat was feeling who said that she felt good after the rest. After the news, they got up to make their way into the kitchen.

They ate their dinner and Pat took her medication afterwards. Pat would have to visit the out-patients at the hospital and see Dr Kelly there. She would have to see him on Monday of next week. Today was Wednesday. Pat could only finish half the salmon fillet. It would be a time before her appetite was restored to her. After dinner Mrs Fitzsimmons washed up. Pat was seated on the sofa listening to a wonderful concert of a Brahms symphony. They both listened to it attentively.

By 10, it was time for bed. Pat got up together with Mrs Fitzsimmons who went up and opened the bedroom door allowing Pat to enter it. Mrs Fitzsimmons drew the curtains and re-arranged the pillows. She said "goodnight, I hope you sleep well and long." She closed the door and made her own way back to her bedroom.

She had checked the doors and windows and everything was locked. She knew it would not be long before Pat recovered fully. She turned off the side light by her bed and went under the covers to go to sleep. Outside it was a mild evening with a moon peering down on earth. Peace had been restored to Pat and she would sleep well tonight.

CHAPTER 15

Kevin and Theresa saw each other once every other week. In the beginning they had a platonic relationship. More recently it had become more intimate. Kevin had slowly fallen in love with Theresa. For Theresa she never thought of marriage to Kevin but a fling. Their love affair was almost complete.

That Sunday Theresa had the day off and she, Kevin, Jane and Gary had a picnic lunch in Regents park. They brought blankets which they spread on the ground and put their picnic baskets on the grass. There was champagne, white wine and bottles of mineral water offered by Jane and Gary. To eat, there was a quiche Theresa had made and tea sandwiches which the café provided located around the corner from Theresa's flat. There was fruit and the year's first strawberries offered by Kevin. The sun shone that May day but when it clouded over, they all put on their anoraks.

Gary proposed to me in the underground exclaimed Jane. It was just before Christmas. I was so surprised I had to ask him to repeat the question "Will you marry me." Finally I told him "yes" and we kissed each other in the open with everyone in the compartment looking on, "she said. The passengers all clapped their hands like an audience in a theatre and wished us both well. We went to our favourite restaurant that night and celebrated. We rang my parents who were surprised by the news. They invited us down to the Manor that week-end.

Gary was a doctor of medicine. He had studied at London University. He had graduated some twelve years earlier. He met Jane at a Christmas party held by a mutual friend of theirs. Upon meeting her, he knew she was the one for him.

It was love at first sight. Three years later they married. He had purchased the house in Wimbledon about a year ago and they had slowly done it up. Before, they rented a flat in the same borough which was trouble free. He worked as a private practitioner in Wimbledon in a surgery not far from home. He had a good friend another doctor called Dr Marsh. Often they shared patients because of the overload of work.

When he met the Gibsons, he was impressed by their friendliness and generous hospitality. It wouldn't be long before they became the best of friends.

Over the week-end when they were at the Manor, he offered Jane an engagement ring made up of an emerald in the centre surrounded by small facets of diamonds. It was quite a large stone which he had purchased in Colombia, South America, on a visit there some years before on a group holiday. The group had been shown the vaults of this jewel which were all available for sale. The emerald was a perfect colour. Gary had taken the stone to Tiffany's jewelry shop in Bond Street and had them design the engagement ring. It was perfectly set and the diamonds couldn't have been more beautiful. Jane was thrilled with it and Alan and Georgia were very impressed. They were most. taken aback by Gary's generosity and taste. It had cost a bit of money but Gary had been saving for years and could afford it. Jane kept the ring on for the rest of the evening.

She was very happy that night.

All this was related to Theresa and Kevin. It gave Kevin ideas about how to propose marriage and what sort of ring he should chose for the bride-to-be.

Kevin would be visiting the Manor in a month's time. Alan and Georgia were hoping for warmer and sunnier weather. They chose early June to have him visit them. Until then, he would look forward to seeing Theresa who had become his closest friend in London besides Roger, a French diplomat working at the Embassy. He played cards with him and two others often getting together for a game of bridge.

CHAPTER 16

Alan and Georgia made their last minute plan for their trip to Japan.

They were leaving that week-end in early March for Tokyo. Kevin had already sent them all the travel documents and vouchers for their stay in the various hotels they were to stay in. In Tokyo they were planning on staying at the Minamo Hotel, a five star hotel. They were leaving on Sunday. Today, Friday, Georgia had bought various useful and wearable travel clothes and Alan had bought a new anorak. All was set and they were almost ready to go.

They were going to phone Jane and Gary to say goodbye to them before they left. The flight would be from Heathrow in the morning arriving in Tokyo the next day. They were both excited about the trip and made sure their iphone chargers were taken with them with the adaptor.

They had been told that people didn't dress up much when going out to dinner. Georgia bought one or two evening cocktail dresses in the event she might need it. Their maid was busy ironing out their clothes to put into their cases.

Their first stop would be Kyoto followed by a stop over for two days in Nara. They would go by car service to Nikko where they would see the famous mausoleum of Ieyasu Tokugawa Head of the Shogunate. They would stay in Nikko for two days followed by a car ride to Aizu Wakamatsu, where they would see the castle and fortress of the Matsudaira family. They would leave in three days from there. They would take the bullet train back to Tokyo. Later they would fly south to visit Naoshima Island to see the Modern Art Museum both Japanese and Western. The weather would be warmer there. Georgia didn't forget her little sun hat. It would be an extensive trip lasting three weeks. Their last journey would be back to Tokyo where they would relax and go shopping in the Ginza in the department stores. At the Minama Hotel, they could eat Japanese food or Western food. Their food was renowned and Alan and Georgia could finally relax for a few days while sightseeing and shopping in Tokyo, before departing

Alan and Geoegia bought a silk kimono cum dressing gown for their daughter Jane. They bought Gary a very handsome yukata or dressing gown for men. They found these things with an English speaking guide who showed them the shops. For herself she chose a beautiful jacket to wear with trousers or skirts. Alan chose a yukata for himself which he looked forward to wearing in the summer months. It was a lightweight cotton robe with a cotton obi to tie it together. The afternoon saw them finishing off their shopping before returning to the hotel and spending the evening in a local Japanese restaurant.

It had been quite an exhausting trip but fascinating, holding interest all the way. They had taken many photos which they would treasure and put into a photo album. They were to leave for London the next day in the afternoon. They still had packing to do and to buy mochi for the children of their neighbour.

They had Kevin to thank for a holiday that went beautifully. All the reservations for the trains and hotels had gone smoothly. Yes, they would invite Kevin back to the Manor once they got back to England.

CHAPTER 17

Kevin had invited Theresa to the Grill Room in one of the leading hotels of London in the West End. Theresa had agreed to the meeting. They met at the lobby of the Beresford Hotel and went directly to the Dining Room.

Kevin was excited that evening and was going to propose to Theresa after they had eaten.

Kevin then popped the question and had taken out of his jacket pocket a small white box. Theresa looked very surprised and said: "I cannot marry you. Although I have great affection for you, my job would not allow me to marry you. You see, I was the one who stole the documents from your briefcase the night we dined with the Gibsons at the Manor. I work for the Government and they wanted your documents. They particularly wanted information about Cardinal Brennan and Father Doughty. They wanted to know how far their summit would agree to letting priests marry. Oh Kevin, I'm so sorry. But you see now, don't you that I cannot marry you."

"We can always try to overlook this flaw in our relationship" said Kevin. "I would do anything to have you my wife. But what you say is that you cannot be trusted with me and I can understand your feelings. Well, maybe the next time, I'll be luckier" he said grimly.

Putting the little box away in his jacket pocket, they eventually rose from the table and made their way out of the dining room. Theresa put her wrap on her shoulder and Kevin led her out of the hotel. The doorman called the cab and they got in together.

It would be a long time before they met again. Little did Kevin know that he was being spied on by Theresa and her spies. Over the week-end he would be visiting the Manor and see the Gibsons again. Jane and Gary would be there. Probably Theresa would not be there. His heart sank at the loss of Theresa but it was best that contact was lost. Soon it would be Christmas and the festive season. He would be with someone else who would help him forget her.

Two years have passed since I last saw or spoke to Theresa. I was on my way home from work, when my phone rang. I took the call and to my surprise it was Theresa. She explained that she had been involved in a car accident and that she was suffering from bruised ribs and a bad neck. The car had been written off. She explained that the accident had happened in the South of France. The driver had suffered a few minor injuries. They had been lucky not to have got killed. Theresa stayed in a rented villa with friends and after a visit to the hospital had returned to the villa. She said she wanted to see me. How about tonight at our favourite restaurant? I said."Alright, that would be good" she said.

We spent an agreeable evening together like old times and caught up on each other's news. She told me she had been invited to the Manor for dinner over the week-end and asked me if I would be there. I told her I had not been invited.

After dinner, I took her back to her flat. She wanted to see me again.

What made Theresa get back in touch with me seems a mystery. I put it down to the car accident. Death had escaped her. It may also have done something to her mind that made her phone me. Whatever it was, it was fortunate we met up again briefly.

I can't say what the future holds in store for us, but for the present, I am happy having a friendly relationship with Theresa. I have another girlfriend now. I still think Cathy is a lovely girl.

www.ingramcontent.com/pod-product-compliance
Lightning Source LLC
LaVergne TN
LVHW050026080526
838202LV00069B/6928